HORSE & BUGGY

BY

ON ICE!

Ethan Long

I Like to Read®

HOLIDAY HOUSE • NEW YORK

Yes, I am.

I am very good.

Look!
I can spin!

You will fall!

I will

Look at this!

Oh, no.

Look at me!

I can't.

Shick
Shick
Shick

Shick
Shick
Shick

Shick
Shick
Shick

Are you ready?

Let's skate!

Library of Congress Cataloging-in-Publication is available.

ISBN: 978-0-8234-4768-8 (hardcover)